Annabelle at the SOUTH POLE

R. W. Alley

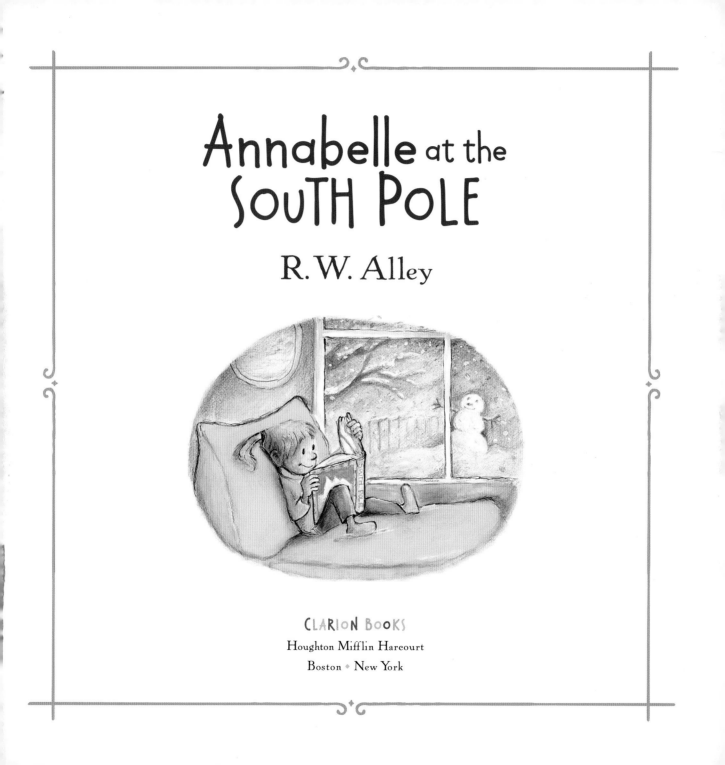

CLARION BOOKS

Houghton Mifflin Harcourt

Boston • New York

Clarion Books
3 Park Avenue
New York, New York 10016

Clarion Books is an imprint of Houghton Mifflin Harcourt Publishing Company.

www.hmhco.com

The illustrations in this book were done in ink, pencils, watercolors,
gouaches, and acrylics on Bristol board paper.
The text was set in Julius Primary.

Library of Congress Cataloging-in-Publication Data
Names: Alley, R. W., 1955-
Title: Annabelle at the South Pole / R. W. Alley.
Description: Boston ; New York : Clarion Books, Houghton Mifflin Harcourt, [2016] | Summary:
"Annabelle tries to escape from her twin brother, Mitchell, and younger siblings, Clark and Gretchen,
on a winter's day by venturing out into the snowy South Pole"—Provided by publisher.
Identifiers: LCCN 2015020437 | ISBN 9780547907048 (hardcover)
Subjects: | CYAC: Snow—Fiction. | Brothers and sisters—Fiction. | Play—Fiction.
Classification: LCC PZ7.A4393 An 2016 | DDC [E]—dc23
LC record available at http://lccn.loc.gov/2015020437

Manufactured in China
SCP 10 9 8 7 6 5 4 3 2 1
4500600822

With love to Z & C & M for
making my world so colorful

ONE snowy day, Mitchell said,
"Behold, I am the Wizard of the World!"
"Look! A scheming sorceress in her tower," said Clark.
"Save my roly-polys from her evil spells!" said Gretchen.

"ZAPSNAZZLE!" said Mitchell.

"You are under my power!"

"Leave me alone," said Annabelle.

"I'm going to the South Pole."

"No one escapes the Wizard of the World!" said Mitchell.

"Watch me," said Annabelle.

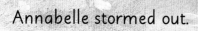

Annabelle stormed out.

Suddenly the Antarctic was everywhere.
But where was the South Pole?

Annabelle stared into the blizzard.
Horrors!
It was the Abominable Snow Giant!

But Annabelle was not scared.

She knew what to do.

"Oh, my," said Annabelle.

"Ouch," said the Abominable Snow Giant.

"Promise to be a good Snow Giant?" said Annabelle.

"I promise," said the Snow Giant.

"I'm going to the South Pole," said Annabelle.
"I know the way," said the Snow Giant.

Horrors! What's this?
The Wizard of the World
and his gang
had gotten there first.

They sang a bubbly spell.

"ZAMZIZZLE, SNOWSIZZLE!"

"Beware of my hot, chocolatey potion!"
said the Wizard of the World.
"I will melt the South Pole!
The world will go all topsy-turvy!"

"Too hot!" said the Snow Giant.

But Annabelle was not afraid.
"Your spell stinks!"
In one ginormous gulp,
Annabelle made the potion vanish!
The South Pole was saved.

"Curses," said the Wizard of the World.
"I am defeated."
"Your spell stunk, but your potion is tasty.
And chocolatey," said Annabelle.
"Thanks, Wizard.

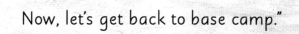
Now, let's get back to base camp."

Back home, there was more
hot chocolate for everyone.